TOM THUMB
AND
OTHER FAVORITES

THE GROLIER SOCIETY INC. • NEW YORK

Contents

With Drawings by
L. Leslie Brooke

TOM THUMB

LONG ago, in the merry days of good King Arthur, there lived a ploughman and his wife. They were very poor, but would have been contented and happy if only they could have had a little child. One day, having

heard of the great fame of the magician Merlin, who was living at the Court of King Arthur, the wife persuaded her husband to go and tell him of their trouble. Having arrived at the Court, the man besought Merlin with tears in his eyes to give them a child, saying that they would be

quite content even though it should be no bigger than his thumb. Merlin determined to grant the request, and what was the countryman's astonishment to find when he reached home that his wife had a son, who, wonderful to relate, was no bigger than his father's thumb!

The parents were now very happy, and the christening of the little fellow took place with great ceremony. The Fairy Queen, attended by all her company of elves, was present at the feast. She kissed the little child, and, giving it the name of Tom Thumb, told her fairies to fetch the

tailors of her Court, who dressed her little godson according to her orders. His hat was made of a beautiful oak leaf, his shirt of a fine spider's web, and his hose and doublet were of thistledown, his stockings were made with the rind of a delicate green apple, and the garters were two of the

finest little hairs imaginable, plucked from his mother's eyebrows, while his shoes were made of the skin of a little mouse. When he was thus dressed, the Fairy Queen kissed him once more, and, wishing him all good luck, flew off with the fairies to her Court.

As Tom grew older, he became very amusing and full of tricks, so that his mother was afraid to let him out of her sight. One day, while she was making a batter pudding, Tom stood on the edge of the bowl, with a lighted candle in his hand, so that she might see that the pudding was made properly. Unfortunately, however, when her back was turned, Tom fell into the bowl, and his

mother, not missing him, stirred him up in the pudding, tied it in a cloth, and put it into the pot. The batter filled Tom's mouth, and prevented him from calling out, but he had no sooner felt the hot water, than he kicked and struggled so much that the pudding jumped about in the pot, and his mother, thinking the pudding was bewitched, was nearly frightened out of her wits. Pulling it out of the pot, she ran with it to her door, and gave it to a tinker who was passing. He was very thankful for it, and looked forward to having a better dinner than he had enjoyed for many a long day. But his pleasure did not last long, for, as he was getting over a stile, he happened

to sneeze very hard, and Tom, who had been quite quiet inside the pudding for some time, called out at the top of his little voice, " Hallo, Pickens ! " This so terrified the

tinker that he flung away the pudding, and ran off as fast as he could. The pudding was all broken to pieces by the fall, and Tom crept out, covered with batter, and ran

home to his mother, who had been looking everywhere for him, and was delighted to see him again. She gave him a bath in a cup, which soon washed off all the pudding, and he was none the worse for his adventure.

A few days after this, Tom accompanied his mother when she went into the fields to milk the cows, and, fearing he might be blown away by the wind, she tied him to a sow-thistle with a little piece of thread. While she was milking, a cow came by, bit off the thistle, and swallowed up Tom. Poor Tom did not like her big teeth, and called out loudly, " Mother, mother ! " " But where are you,

14

Tommy, my dear Tommy?" cried out his mother, wringing
her hands. "Here, mother," he shouted, "inside the red
cow's mouth!" And, saying that, he began to kick and
scratch till the poor cow was nearly mad, and at length

tumbled him out of her mouth. On seeing this, his mother
rushed to him, caught him in her arms, and carried him
safely home.

Some days after this, his father took him to the fields a-ploughing, and gave him a whip, made of a barley straw, with which to drive the oxen; but little Tom was soon lost in a furrow. An eagle seeing him, picked him up and

flew with him to the top of a hill where stood a giant's castle. The giant put him at once into his mouth, intending to swallow him up, but Tom made such a great disturbance when he got inside that the monster was soon glad to get

rid of him, and threw him far away into the sea. But he was not drowned, for he had scarcely touched the water before he was swallowed by a large fish, which was shortly

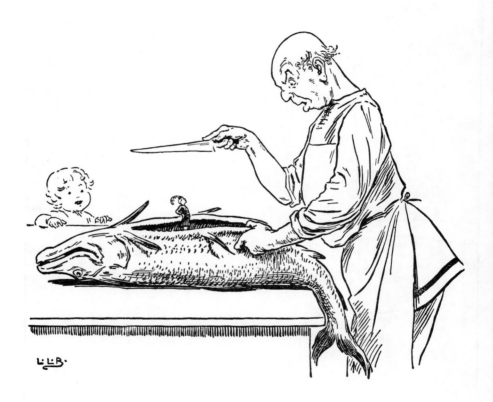

afterwards captured and brought to King Arthur, as a present, by the fisherman. When the fish was opened, everyone was astonished at finding Tom inside. He was

at once carried to the King, who made him his Court dwarf.

> Long time he lived in jollity,
> Beloved of the Court,
> And none like Tom was so esteemed
> Amongst the better sort.

The Queen was delighted with the little boy, and made him dance a gaillard on her left hand. He danced so well that King Arthur gave him a ring, which he wore round his waist like a girdle.

Tom soon began to long to see his parents again, and begged the King to allow him to go home for a short time. This was readily permitted, and the King told him he might take with him as much money as he could carry.

And so away goes lusty Tom,
    With three pence at his back—
A heavy burthen which did make
    His very bones to crack.

He had to rest more than a hundred times by the

way, but, after two days and two nights, he reached his father's house in safety. His mother saw him coming, and ran out to meet him, and there was great rejoicing at his arrival. He spent three happy days at home, and then set out for the Court once more.

Shortly after his return, he one day displeased the King, so, fearing the royal anger, he crept into an empty flower-pot, where he lay for a long time. At last he ventured to peep out, and, seeing a fine large butterfly on the ground close by, he stole out of his hiding-place, jumped on its back, and was carried up into the air. The King and

nobles all strove to catch him, but at last poor Tom fell from his seat into a watering-pot, in which he was almost

drowned, only luckily the gardener's child saw him, and pulled him out. The King was so pleased to have him safe once more that he forgot to scold him, and made much of him instead.

Tom afterwards lived many years at Court, one of the best beloved of King Arthur's knights.

> Thus he at tilt and tournament
>   Was entertained so,
> That all the rest of Arthur's knights
>   Did him much pleasure show.
> With good Sir Launcelot du Lake,
>   Sir Tristram and Sir Guy,
> Yet none compared to brave Tom Thumb
>   In acts of chivalry.

THE THREE BEARS

WITH DRAWINGS BY
L. LESLIE BROOKE

THE STORY OF
THE THREE BEARS

ONCE upon a time there were Three Bears, who lived together in a house of their own, in a wood. One of them was a Little, Small, Wee Bear; and one was a Middle-sized Bear, and the other was a Great, Huge Bear. They had each a pot for their porridge; a little pot for the Little, Small, Wee Bear; and a middle-sized pot for the Middle Bear, and a great pot for the Great, Huge

Bear. And they had each a chair to sit in; a little chair for the Little, Small, Wee Bear; and a middle-sized chair for the Middle Bear, and a great chair for the Great,

Huge Bear. And they had each a bed to sleep in; a little bed for the Little, Small, Wee Bear; and a middle-sized bed for the Middle Bear, and a great bed for the Great, Huge Bear.

One day, after they had made the porridge for their breakfast, and poured it into their porridge-pots, they walked out into the wood while the porridge was cooling, that they might not burn their mouths by beginning too

soon to eat it. And while they were walking, a little Girl
called Goldenlocks came to the house. First she looked in
at the window, and then she peeped in at the keyhole;
and seeing nobody in the house, she turned the handle of

the door. The door was not fastened, because the Bears
were good Bears, who did nobody any harm, and never
suspected that anybody would harm them. So Goldenlocks
opened the door, and went in; and well pleased she was

when she saw the porridge on the table. If she had been
a thoughtful little Girl, she would have waited till the
Bears came home, and then, perhaps, they would have
asked her to breakfast; for they were good Bears — a little

rough or so, as the manner of Bears is, but for all that very good-natured and hospitable. But the porridge looked tempting, and she set about helping herself.

So first she tasted the porridge of the Great, Huge Bear, and that was too hot for her. And then she tasted the porridge of the Middle Bear, and that was too cold for her. And then she went to the porridge of the Little, Small, Wee Bear, and tasted that; and that was neither too hot nor too cold, but just right, and she liked it so well that she ate it all up.

Then Goldenlocks sat down in the chair of the Great, Huge Bear, and that was too hard for her. And then she sat down in the chair of the Middle Bear, and that was too soft for her. And then she sat down in the chair of the Little, Small, Wee Bear, and that was neither too hard nor too soft, but just right. So she seated herself in it, and there she sat till the bottom of the chair came out, and down she came plump upon the ground.

Then Goldenlocks went upstairs into the bed-chamber in which the three Bears slept. And first she lay down upon the bed of the Great, Huge Bear, but that was too high at the head for her. And next she lay down upon the bed of the Middle Bear, and that was too high at the foot for her. And then she lay down upon the bed of the Little, Small, Wee Bear; and that was neither too high at

the head nor at the foot, but just right. So she covered
herself up comfortably, and lay there till she fell fast asleep.

By this time the Three Bears thought their porridge
would be cool enough; so they came home to breakfast.
Now Goldenlocks had left the spoon of the Great, Huge
Bear standing in his porridge.

"SOMEBODY HAS BEEN AT MY PORRIDGE!"
said the Great, Huge Bear, in his great, rough, gruff voice.

And when the Middle Bear looked at hers, she saw that
the spoon was standing in it too.

"SOMEBODY HAS BEEN AT MY PORRIDGE!"
said the Middle Bear, in her middle voice. Then the

Little, Small, Wee Bear looked at his, and there was the
spoon in the porridge-pot, but the porridge was all gone.

"SOMEBODY HAS BEEN AT MY PORRIDGE, AND HAS EATEN IT ALL UP!"
said the Little, Small, Wee Bear, in his little, small, wee
voice.

Upon this the Three Bears, seeing that someone had entered their house, and eaten up the Little, Small, Wee Bear's breakfast, began to look about them. Now Golden-locks had not put the hard cushion straight when she rose from the chair of the Great, Huge Bear.

"SOMEBODY HAS BEEN SITTING IN MY CHAIR!" said the Great, Huge Bear, in his great, rough, gruff voice.

And Goldenlocks had squatted down the soft cushion of the Middle Bear.

"SOMEBODY HAS BEEN SITTING IN MY CHAIR!" said the Middle Bear, in her middle voice.

And you know what Goldenlocks had done to the third chair.

"SOMEBODY HAS BEEN SITTING IN MY CHAIR, AND HAS SAT THE BOTTOM OUT OF IT!" said the Little, Small, Wee Bear, in his little, small, wee voice.

Then The Three Bears thought it necessary that they
should make farther search; so they went upstairs into their
bedchamber. Now Goldenlocks had pulled the pillow of
the Great, Huge Bear out of its place.

"SOMEBODY HAS BEEN LYING IN MY BED!"
said the Great, Huge Bear, in his great, rough, gruff voice.

And Goldenlocks had pulled the bolster of the Middle
Bear out of its place.

"SOMEBODY HAS BEEN LYING IN MY BED!"
said the Middle Bear, in her middle voice.

And when the Little, Small, Wee Bear came to look
at his bed, there was the bolster in its place; and the
pillow in its place upon the bolster; and upon the pillow
was the head of Goldenlocks — which was not in its place,
for she had no business there.

"SOMEBODY HAS BEEN LYING IN MY BED—AND HERE SHE IS!"
said the Little, Small, Wee Bear, in his little, small, wee
voice.

Goldenlocks had heard in her sleep the great, rough, gruff voice of the Great, Huge Bear, and the middle

voice of the Middle Bear, but it was only as if she had heard someone speaking in a dream. But when she heard

the little, small, wee voice of the Little, Small, Wee Bear, it was so sharp, and so shrill, that it awakened her at once. Up she started; and when she saw the Three Bears on one side of the bed she tumbled herself out at the other, and ran to the window. Now the window was open, because the Bears, like good, tidy Bears, as they were, always opened their bedchamber window when they got up in the morning. Out Goldenlocks jumped, and ran away as fast as she could run — never looking behind her; and what happened to her afterwards I cannot tell. But the Three Bears never saw anything more of her.

FIDDLE-DE-DEE, fiddle-de-dee,
 The fly shall marry the humble-bee.
They went to the church, and married was she:
The fly has married the humble-bee.

MISTRESS MARY, quite contrary,
How does your garden grow?
With cockle-shells, and silver bells,
And pretty maids all a row.

THE lion and the unicorn
   Were fighting for the crown;
The lion beat the unicorn
   All round about the town.

Some gave them white bread,
   And some gave them brown;
Some gave them plum-cake,
   And sent them out of town.

THERE was a crooked man, and he went a
    crooked mile;
He found a crooked sixpence against a crooked stile:
He bought a crooked cat, which caught a crooked
    mouse,
And they all lived together in a little crooked house.

L ITTLE Tommy Tittlemouse
Lived in a little house;
He caught fishes
In other men's ditches.

I HAD a little hen, the prettiest ever seen;
   She washed me the dishes, and kept the house
   clean;
She went to the mill to fetch me some flour;
She brought it home in less than an hour;
She baked me my bread, she brewed me my ale;
She sat by the fire, and told many a fine tale.

JACK SPRAT could eat no fat;
  His wife could eat no lean:
And so, betwixt them both, you see
  They licked the platter clean.

I F all the world was apple-pie,
 And all the sea was ink,
And all the trees were bread and cheese,
 What should we have for drink?

THE man in the wilderness asked me
How many strawberries grew in the sea.
I answered him as I thought good,
As many red herrings grew in the wood.

PUSSY-CAT, pussy-cat, where have you been?
    I've been up to London to look at the queen.
Pussy-cat, pussy-cat, what did you there?
I frightened a little mouse under the chair.

A TREASURY
OF
NURSERY RHYMES

ILLUSTRATED BY
CHARLES ROBINSON

THE GROLIER SOCIETY INC. • NEW YORK

Contents

A MEDLEY

O N Christmas Eve I turned the spit,
I burnt my fingers, I feel it yet;
The cock sparrow flew over the table,
The pot began to play with the ladle;
The ladle stood up like a naked man,
And vowed he 'd fight the frying-pan;
The frying-pan behind the door
Said he never saw the like before;
And the kitchen clock I was going to wind
Said he never saw the like behind.

THE WISE MEN OF GOTHAM

Three wise men of Gotham
They went to sea in a bowl;
And if the bowl had been stronger,
My song had been longer.

THE ♥ ♥
QUEEN *of*
HEARTS

The Queen of Hearts she
made some tarts,

All on a summer's day;

The Knave of Hearts he stole those
tarts,

And took them clean away.

The Queen of Hearts

The King of Hearts
called for those
tarts,

And beat the
Knave full
sore.

The Knave of Hearts

       brought back those tarts,

And vowed he 'd steal no more.

T° MARKET

To market, to market,
   To buy a fat pig;
Home again, home again,
   Jiggety jig.

To market, to market,
   To buy a fat hog;
Home again, home again,
   Jiggety jog.

9

Cock-a-doodle--do

COCK-A-DOODLE-DO

Cock-a-doodle-do!
My dame has lost her shoe;
My master's lost his fiddle-stick,
And don't know what to do.

Cock-a-doodle-do!
What is my dame to do?
Till master finds his fiddle-stick,
She'll dance without her shoe.

Tom, Tom, the Piper's Son

TOM, THE PIPER'S SON

Tom, Tom, the piper's son,
Stole a pig and away he run!
The pig was eat and Tom was beat,
And Tom went howling down the street.

13

THE WIND

When the wind is in the East,
'T is neither good for man nor beast;
When the wind is in the North,
The skilful fisher goes not forth;
When the wind is in the South,
It blows the bait in the fish's mouth;
When the wind is in the West,
Then 't is at the very best.

HUMPTY-DUMPTY

UMPTY-DUMPTY sat on a wall,
Humpty-Dumpty had a great fall;

Threescore men, and threescore more,
Cannot place Humpty-Dumpty as he
was before.

WHAT ARE LITTLE BOYS MADE OF?

What are little boys made of, made of?
What are little boys made of?
Snips and snails, and puppy-dogs' tails;
That's what little boys are made
of, made of.

What are little girls made of,
made of?
What are little girls made of?
Sugar and spice, and all things nice,
That's what little girls are made
of, made of.

15

A FROG HE WOULD A·WOOING GO

A frog he would a-wooing go,
      Heigho! says Rowley,
Whether his mother would let him or no.
    With a rowley powley, gammon and spinach,
    Heigho! says Anthony Rowley.

17

So off he set with his
    opera hat,
Heigho! says Rowley,
And on the road he
    met with a rat.
With a rowley powley,
    gammon and spinach,
Heigho! says Anthony
    Rowley.

"Pray, Mr. Rat, will
    you go with me?"
Heigho! says Rowley,
"Kind Mistress Mous-
    ey for to see!"
With a rowley powley,
    gammon and spinach,
Heigho! says Anthony
    Rowley.

When they reached the
    door of Mousey's hall,
Heigho! says Rowley,
They gave a loud knock,
    and they gave a loud
    call.
With a rowley powley,
    gammon and spinach,
Heigho! says Anthony
    Rowley.

" Pray, Mistress Mouse, are
you within?"
  Heigho! says Rowley;
" Oh, yes, kind sirs, I 'm sit-
ting to spin."
    With a rowley powley,
      gammon and spinach,
Heigho! says Anthony Rowley.

" Pray, Mistress Mouse, will
you give us some beer?"
  Heigho! says Rowley,
" For Froggy and I are fond
of good cheer."
    With a rowley powley,
      gammon and spinach,
Heigho! says Anthony Rowley.

" Pray, Mr. Frog, will you
give us a song?"
  Heigho! says Rowley;
" But let it be something that 's
not very long."
    With a rowley powley,
      gammon and spinach,
Heigho! says Anthony Rowley.

" Indeed, Mistress Mouse,"
replied Mr. Frog,
  Heigho! says Rowley,
" A cold has made me as
hoarse as a hog."
    With a rowley powley,
      gammon and spinach,
Heigho! says Anthony Rowley.

A Frog he would a-wooing go

"Since you have caught cold, Mr. Frog," Mousey said,
    Heigho! says Rowley,
"I 'll sing you a song that I
    have just made."
    With a rowley powley,
        gammon and spinach,
Heigho! says Anthony Rowley.

But while they were all a merry-
    making,
    Heigho! says Rowley,
A cat with her kittens came
    tumbling in.
    With a rowley powley,
        gammon and spinach,
Heigho! says Anthony Rowley.

The cat she seized
    the rat by the crown,
    Heigho! says Rowley,
The kittens they pulled
    the little mouse down.
    With a rowley powley, gam-
        mon and spinach,
Heigho! says Anthony Rowley.

This put Mr. Frog in a
  terrible fright,
    Heigho! says Rowley;
He took up his hat and he
  wished them good-night.
    With a rowley powley,
      gammon and spinach,
Heigho! says Anthony Rowley.

But as Froggy was crossing
  over a brook,
    Heigho! says Rowley,
A lily-white duck came and
  gobbled him up.
    With a rowley powley,
      gammon and spinach,
Heigho! says Anthony Rowley.

So there was an end of one, two, and three,
    Heigho! says Rowley,
The Rat, the Mouse, and the little Frog-gee!
    With a rowley powley, gammon and spinach,
    Heigho! says Anthony Rowley.

GOOD KING ARTHUR

WHEN good King Arthur ruled this
land
He was a goodly king;
He stole three pecks of barley-meal
To make a bag-pudding.

Good King Arthur

A bag-pudding the
         king did make,
And stuff'd it well
              with plums;

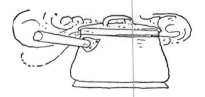

Good King Arthur

And in it put great lumps of fat,
　　As big as my two thumbs.

The king and queen did eat thereof,
　　And noble men beside;
And what they could not eat that night,
　　The queen next morning fried.

SOLOMON GRUNDY

OLOMON GRUNDY,
    Born on a Monday,
    Christened on Tuesday,
    Married on Wednesday,
    Took ill on Thursday,
    Worse on Friday,
    Died on Saturday,
    Buried on Sunday,
    This is the end
    Of Solomon Grundy.

THREE BLIND MICE

Three blind mice, three blind mice,
They all ran after the
    farmer's wife,
She cut off their tails with
    a carving knife;
Did you ever see such a
    thing in your life
As three blind mice?

25

CROSS-PATCH

CROSS-PATCH, draw the latch,
    Sit by the fire and spin;
Take a cup, and drink it up,
    Then call your neighbours in.

YANKEE DOODLE

Yankee Doodle came to town,
    Mounted on a pony;
He stuck a feather in his cap
    And called it Maccaroni.

Yankee Doodle came to town,
    Yankee Doodle dandy,
He stuck a feather in his cap
    And called it sugar-candy.

TWINKLE, twinkle, little star,
    How I wonder what you are!

Twinkle, twinkle, little Star

Up above the world so high,
Like a diamond in the sky.

When the blazing sun is gone,
When he nothing shines upon,
Then you show your little light,
Twinkle, twinkle, all the night.

Then the traveller in the dark
Thanks you for your tiny spark:
How could he see where to go,
If you did not twinkle so?

In the dark blue sky you keep,
Often through my curtains peep,
For you never shut your eye
Till the sun is in the sky.

How your bright and tiny spark
Lights the traveller in the dark!
Though I know not what you are,
Twinkle, twinkle, little star.

TOAD AND FROG

"Croak," said the toad, "I'm hungry I think,
To-day I've had nothing to eat or to drink;
I'll crawl to a garden and jump through the pales,
And there I'll dine nicely on slugs and on snails."

"Ho, ho!" quoth the frog, "is that what you mean?
Then I'll hop away to the next meadow stream,
There I will drink, and eat worms and slugs too,
And then I shall have a good dinner like you."

LITTLE JACK HORNER

Little Jack Horner
Sat in a corner
Eating of Christmas pie;

He put in his thumb,
And pulled out a plum,
And cried "What a good boy was I!"

THERE WAS A LITTLE MAN

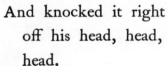

THERE was a little man, and
he had a little gun,

And his bullets they were
made of lead, lead, lead.

He shot Johnny Sprig through
the middle of his wig,

And knocked it right
off his head, head,
head.

HEY! DIDDLE, DIDDLE

HEY! diddle, diddle,
  The cat and the fiddle,
  The cow jumped over the moon;
  The little dog laughed
  To see such craft,
  And the dish ran away with the
    spoon.

TWO LITTLE BIRDS

There were two blackbirds
  Sat upon a hill,
The one named Jack,
  The other named Jill.
    Fly away, Jack!
    Fly away, Jill!
    Come again, Jack!
    Come again, Jill!

SING A SONG of SIXPENCE

ING a song of sixpence,
  Pockets full of rye;
Four and twenty black-
    birds
  Baked in a pie.

When the pie was opened
  The birds began to
    sing;
Was not that a dainty dish
  To set before the king?

The king was in his counting-
house

Counting out his money;

The queen was in the parlour,

Eating bread and honey;

Sing a Song of Sixpence

The maid was in the garden
Hanging out the clothes,
Down came a blackbird,
And snapped off her nose.

The Old Woman who lived in a Shoe

THE OLD WOMAN WHO LIVED IN A SHOE

THERE was an old woman who lived in a shoe,

She had so many children she didn't know what to do;

She gave them some broth without any bread,

Then whipped them all round, and sent them to bed.

BUTTONS

BUTTONS, a farthing a pair,

Come, who will buy them of me?

They 're round and sound and pretty,

And fit for the girls of the city.

Come, who will buy them of me,

Buttons, a farthing a pair?

SULKY SUE

Here 's Sulky Sue;

What shall we do?

Turn her face to the wall

Till she comes to.

A DILLER, A DOLLAR

A diller, a dollar,
A ten o'clock scholar;
What makes you come so soon?
You used to come at ten o'clock,
But now you come at noon.

Three Jolly Welshmen

Three Jolly Welshmen.

There were three jolly Welshmen,
　　As I have heard say,
And they went a-hunting
　　Upon St. David's day.

All the day they hunted,
　　And nothing could they find;

But a ship a-sailing,
    A-sailing with the wind.

One said it was a ship,
    The other he said " Nay ";
The third he said it was a house,
    With the chimney blown away.

And all the night they hunted,
    And nothing could they find,
But the moon a-gliding,
    A-gliding with the wind.

One said it was the moon,
    The other he said " Nay ";
The third he said it was a cheese,
    With half o' it cut away.

THREE MEN IN A TUB

Rub-a-dub-dub,

Three men in a tub;

And who do you think they be?

The butcher, the baker,

The candlestick-maker;

Turn 'em out, knaves all three!

43

CURLY
LOCKS

Thou shalt sit on a
cushion and sew a
fine seam, And feed
upon strawberries
sugar and cream.

CURLY LOCKS

Curly locks! curly locks!
  wilt thou be mine?
Thou shalt not wash dishes,
  nor yet feed the swine;
But sit on a cushion, and
  sew a fine seam,
And feed upon strawberries,
  sugar, and cream!

Little Bo peep

Little Bo-Peep

Little Bo-Peep has lost her sheep,
  And can't tell where to find them;
Let them alone, and they'll come home,
  And bring their tails behind them.

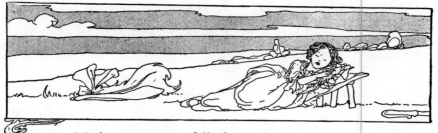

Little Bo-Peep fell fast asleep,
  And dreamt she heard them bleating;
And when she awoke, she found it a joke,
  For still they were all fleeting.

Then up she took her little
   crook,
Determined for to find them;

Little Bo-Peep

She found them indeed, but it made her heart bleed,
    For they'd left all their tails behind them.

It happened one day as Bo-Peep did stray
    Into a meadow hard by,
There she espied their tails side by side,
    All hung on a tree to dry.

Little Bo-Peep

She heaved a sigh, and wiped her eye,
    And went over hill and dale, oh;
And tried what she could, as a shepherdess should,
    To tack to each sheep its tail, oh!

JACK
and
JILL

Jack and Jill
      went up the hill,
To fetch a
      pail of water.

Jack and Jill

Jack fell down, and
broke his crown,

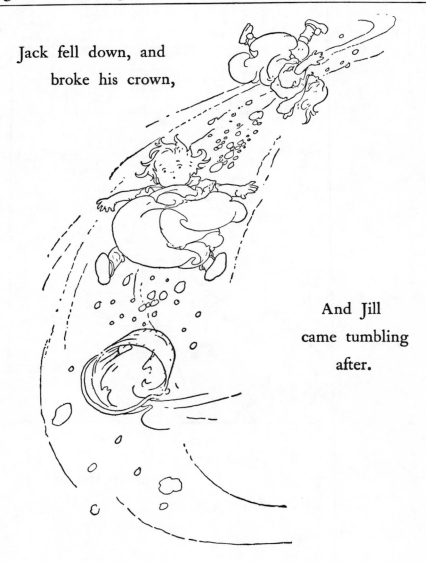

And Jill
came tumbling
after.

Jack and Jill

Then up Jack got,
   and off did trot,
As fast as he
   could caper,

To old Dame Dob,
   who patched his nob,
With vinegar and
   brown paper.

WEE WILLIE WINKIE

EE WILLIE WINKIE runs through the
town,

Up stairs and down stairs, in his night-
gown,

Rapping at the window, crying through
the lock:

"Are the children in their beds, for
it's past eight o'clock."

BAA, BAA, BLACK SHEEP

Baa, baa, black sheep, have you any wool?

Yes, marry, have I, three bags full:

One for my master, one for my dame,

But none for the little boy who cries in the lane.

THE FARMER AND HIS DAUGHTER

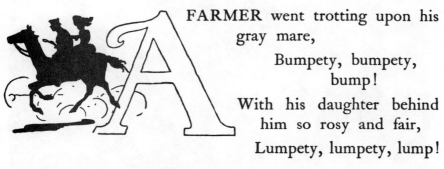

A FARMER went trotting upon his
   gray mare,
      Bumpety, bumpety,
         bump!
With his daughter behind
   him so rosy and fair,
   Lumpety, lumpety, lump!

A raven cried "croak" and they all tumbled down,
      Bumpety, bumpety, bump!
The mare broke her knees, and the farmer his crown,
      Lumpety, lumpety, lump!

The mischievous raven flew laughing away,
      Bumpety, bumpety, bump!
And vowed he would serve them the same the next day,
      Lumpety, lumpety, lump!

Simple Simon

SIMPLE SIMON

SIMPLE SIMON met a pie-man,
    Going to the fair;
Says Simple Simon to the pie-man,
    " Let me taste your ware."

Says the pie-man unto Simon,
    " First give me a penny."
Says Simple Simon to the pie-man,
    " I have not got any."

He went to catch a dicky-bird,
    And thought he could not fail,
Because he had got a little salt
    To put upon his tail.

Simple Simon

He went to
ride a
spotted cow,

That had got
a little
calf,

She threw him
down upon
the ground,

Which made
the people
laugh.

Simple Simon

Then Simple Simon went a-hunting,
    For to catch a hare,
He rode a goat about the street,
    But could not find one there.

He went for to eat honey
    Out of the mustard-pot,
He bit his tongue until he cried,
    That was all the good he got.

Simple Simon

SIMPLE SIMON went a-fishing
  For to catch a whale;
 And all the water he had got
  Was in his mother's pail.

 He went to take a bird's nest,
  Was built upon a bough;
A branch gave way, and Simon fell
  Into a dirty slough.

He went to shoot a
 wild duck,
 But the wild duck
  flew away;
Says Simon, "I can't
 hit him,
 Because he will not
  stay."

Simple Simon

NCE Simon made a great
   Snowball,
   And brought it in to roast;
He laid it down before the
   fire,
   And soon the ball was lost.

HE went to slide upon the ice,
   Before the ice would bear;
Then he plunged in above his
   knees,
   Which made poor Simon stare.

He went to try if cherries ripe
   Grew upon a thistle;
He pricked his finger very much,
   Which made poor Simon whistle.

Simple Simon

He washed himself with blacking-ball,
    Because he had no soap:
Then, then, said to his mother,
    "I'm a beauty now, I hope."

He went for water in a sieve,
    But soon it all ran through;
And now poor Simple Simon
    Bids you all adieu.

DEEDLE, deedle, dumpling, my son John
Went to bed with his trousers on;
One shoe off, the other shoe on,
Deedle, Deedle, dumpling, my son John.